Margaret Mahy (1936-2012) wrote more than 200 books for children and
is considered one of the outstanding children's writers of the twentieth century.
She received the Hans Christian Andersen Award, the highest international
recognition for children's authors, and twice won the Carnegie Medal. Her picture
books for Frances Lincoln include *Dashing Dog*, illustrated by Sarah Garland, and
Down the Back of the Chair, *Bubble Trouble* and *The Man from the Land
of Fandango*, all illustrated by Polly Dunbar.

Margaret Chamberlain is an internationally bestselling illustrator of
children's books. Her picture books for Frances Lincoln include *Tales from Grimm*,
written by Antonia Barber, *My Two Grannies* and *My Two Grandads*, written by
Floella Benjamin, and *Made by Raffi*, written by Craig Pomranz.
She lives in Dorset.

In loving memory of Margaret Mahy 1936-2012

Brimming with creative inspiration, how-to projects, and useful
information to enrich your everyday life, Quarto Knows is a favourite
destination for those pursuing their interests and passions. Visit our
site and dig deeper with our books into your area of interest:
Quarto Creates, Quarto Cooks, Quarto Homes, Quarto Lives,
Quarto Drives, Quarto Explores, Quarto Gifts, or Quarto Kids.

JANETTA OTTER-BARRY BOOKS

Text copyright © Margaret Mahy 1997
Illustrations copyright © Margaret Chamberlain 2014

First published in Great Britain and the USA in 1997
with illustrations by Patricia McCarthy by Viking Children's Books
This edition first published in Great Britain and in the USA in 2014 by
Frances Lincoln Children's Books,
an imprint of The Quarto Group.
The Old Brewery, 6 Blundell Street, London N7 9BH, United Kingdom.
T (0)20 7700 6700 F (0)20 7700 8066 www.QuartoKnows.com

ISBN 978-0-7112-5400-8

Set in ITC Korinna and Langer

Manufactured in Guangdong, China TT012020

1 3 5 7 9 8 6 4 2

MIX
Paper from
responsible sources
FSC® C016973

BOOM, Baby, BOOM BOOM!

Margaret Mahy

Illustrated by Margaret Chamberlain

Frances Lincoln
Children's Books

"I've made a lovely lunch for you,"
Mama said, popping her baby
into the blue highchair.
"I hope you are
        hungry,
            hungry,
                hungry!"

She did not know that the animals
were listening at the window.

"You have beautiful bread and honey.
You have two lettuce leaves.
You have a sweet apple, peeled and pipped.
You have a piece of cheese,
and a raw carrot – scrubbed clean.
What a lovely lunch for a hungry baby!

And while you eat it all up,
I'll just **biddy-boom-boom**
on my **diddy-dum-drums**.
Beating those drums makes me
feel at ease with the world."

She did not know
that the animals
were listening
at the window.

And so Mama began to beat
on the drums.

Boom-biddy-boom-biddy
Boom Boom Boom.
Closing her eyes, she smiled
as she listened to the beat.

She did not know
that the animals were
scrambling for the door.

The baby looked at her lovely lunch. She picked up the piece of cheese. But she didn't eat it.

Instead, she threw the cheese on the floor.

In crept the yellow cat –
and ate it all up.

Boom-biddy-boom-biddy

MEW-MEW-MEW!

Then the baby picked up the bread and honey.
She leaned sideways in her blue highchair

and threw the bread

and honey on the floor.

In lolloped the brown dog
with the ginger eyebrows –
and ate it all up.

Boom-biddy-boom-biddy

BOW-WOW-WOW!

Then the baby threw the slices
of sweet apple on the floor.

In scuttled the hens and the red rooster
in their yellow stockings –
chuckling and clucking –
and pecked it all up.

Boom-biddy-boom-biddy
COCK-A-DOODLE-DOO!

Then the baby threw

the lettuce on the floor.

In trotted the black-faced sheep
on her high-heeled hooves –
and ate it all up.

Boom-biddy-boom-biddy

BAA-BAA-BAA!

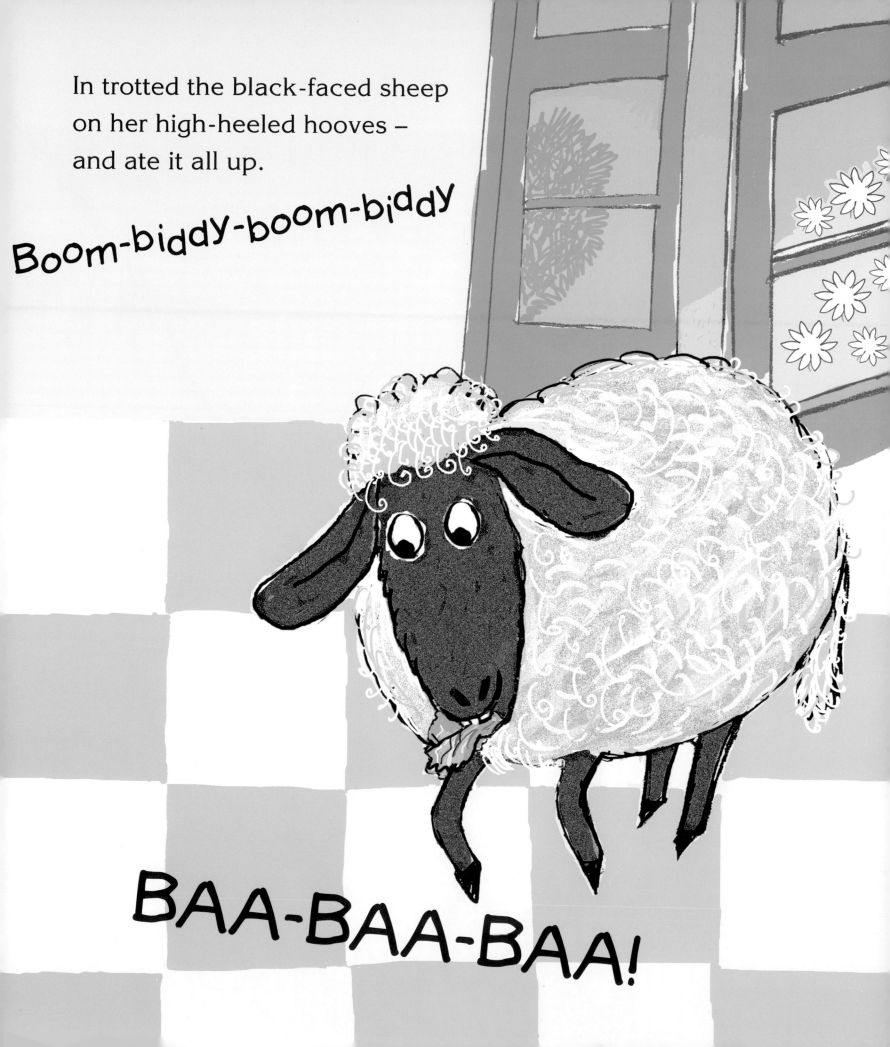

Then the baby threw
the raw carrot on the floor.
In ambled the brown-and-white cow –
and ate it all up.

Boom-biddy-boom-biddy

MOO-MOO-MOO!

Suddenly, Mama stopped
beating the diddy-dum-drums.
There was no more
Boom-biddy-
boom-biddy!

Out ran the CAT!
Out ran the DOG!

Mama sighed with happiness.
Beating those drums made her
feel really at ease with the world.

Out flew the HENS
and the RED ROOSTER!
Out trotted the SHEEP!

Up stood Mama.
One last beat.
One last boom.

Out cantered the brown-and-white COW!

When Mama turned round, the baby
was sitting alone in her highchair.
Her plate was completely empty.

"Oh, you good baby!" cried Mama.
"You've eaten every bit and bite
of your lunch. Listening to my
Boom-biddy-Boom-Boom
beat must make you
hungry,
hungry,
hungry!

Then she hugged and kissed the baby
and gave her a banana –
peeled and ready to eat.

And the baby ate it all up.

Boom-biddy-boom-biddy

YUM-YUM-YUM!

MORE PICTURE BOOKS BY MARGARET MAHY
PUBLISHED BY FRANCES LINCOLN CHILDREN'S BOOKS

978-1-84507-602-3

Down the Back of the Chair
Illustrated by Polly Dunbar

"Exuberant rhyming story celebrating the chaos of everyday life and the power of the imagination."
– *Independent on Sunday*

"This simple story zips along and the language really fizzes" – *Daily Telegraph*

978-1-84780-186-9

Bubble Trouble
Illustrated by Polly Dunbar

"A fabulous bouncing story told in a rollicking rhyme" – *Julia Eccleshare, Lovereading*

"A joy to read aloud, and gorgeously illustrated" – *Bookseller*

978-1-84780-474-7

The Man from the Land of Fandango
Illustrated by Polly Dunbar

"Everything a child needs in a book – colour, imagination and glorious life" – *Carousel*

Frances Lincoln titles are available from all good bookshops.
You can also buy books and find out more about your favourite titles,
authors and illustrators on our website: www.franceslincoln.com